3.50

P9-CJR-000

Forensic Crime Solvers

Earth Evidence

By Michael Martin

Consultant:
Raymond Murray, PhD
Author, *Evidence from the Earth: Forensic Geology and Criminal Investigation*

Capstone
press ®

Mankato, Minnesota

Edge Books are published by Capstone Press,
151 Good Counsel Drive, P.O. Box 669, Mankato, Minnesota 56002.
www.capstonepress.com

Library of Congress Cataloging-in-Publication Data
Martin, Michael, 1948–
    Earth evidence / by Michael Martin.
      p. cm. —(Edge books. Forensic crime solvers)
    Includes bibliographical references and index.
    ISBN-13: 978-0-7368-6787-0 (hardcover)
    ISBN-10: 0-7368-6787-2 (hardcover)
    ISBN-13: 978-0-7368-7871-5 (softcover pbk.)
    ISBN-10: 0-7368-7871-8 (softcover pbk.)
      1. Forensic geology—Juvenile literature. 2. Soils—Identification—Juvenile literature.
3. Criminal investigation—Juvenile literature. 4. Evidence, Criminal—Juvenile literature.
I. Title. II. Series.
QE38.5.M37 2007
363.25'62—dc22   2006024765

Summary: Describes how forensic geologists help solve crimes.

Editorial Credits
Angie Kaelberer, editor; Juliette Peters, set designer; Ted Williams, book designer;
    Wanda Winch, photo researcher/photo editor

Photo Credits
Capstone Press/Karon Dubke, 4, 6, 7, 9, 10, 12
Corbis/Bettmann, 22, 24; Reuters, 27
Getty Images Inc./Aurora/Cary Wolinsky, 16; ChinaFotoPress, 1;
    Hulton Archive/New York Times Co., 20; Paul O'Driscoll, 26
iStockphoto Inc./Clay Lipsky, 25
Photodisc, back cover
PhotoEdit Inc./Dwayne Newton, 18; Gary Conner, 14
Raymond C. Murray, author of *Evidence From The Earth: Forensic Geology and
    Criminal Investigation*, Mountain Press, 2004, 13
Shutterstock/Emily Veinglory, front cover; Marek Pawluczuk, 23
SuperStock/age fotostock, 8
Visuals Unlimited/Brad Mogen, 29; Jeffrey Howe, 17

1 2 3 4 5 6 12 11 10 09 08 07

Table of Contents

CHAPTER 1

Learn about:
- Tracks in the mud
- Forensic geologists
- Pebbles of evidence

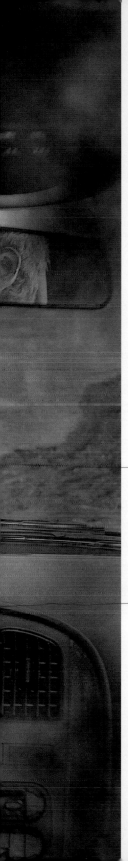

Mud and Murder

Jeff Grant walked down a gravel road toward the Apple River. He planned to spend a pleasant day fishing with his dog.

Grant came to a boat landing and noticed a van parked nearby. Its back windows were shattered. A man sat slumped behind the wheel. Wet, sticky blood dripped down the back of his head.

Grant called police on his cell phone. The police arrived, followed by a medical examiner (ME) and two crime scene investigators (CSIs). They found that the man had been shot through the head.

Tracks of a Killer?

The CSIs searched for clues near the van. Heavy rain had fallen the night before, turning the ground into a sea of mud. Deep tire tracks were in the soft, spongy ground. It looked as if someone had left in a hurry.

◄ Fisherman Jeff Grant made a terrifying discovery at a boat landing.

The CSIs took about 100 photos of the crime scene. They also took samples of the soil in the tracks and near the river.

The police learned the dead man had used illegal drugs. He owed a large amount of money to a drug dealer. The police believed the drug dealer had shot the man. But the dealer lived in a city 60 miles (97 kilometers) away. He said he had never been to that part of the state.

The tire tracks were easy to see in the wet, muddy ground.

A CSI took samples of soil near the river.

Calling in an Expert

The police examined the drug dealer's car. They found fresh mud spattered on the back fenders and wheels. They asked forensic geologist Abby Baker to examine the mud. Forensic geologists study evidence found in soil, rocks, and other natural elements.

Azurite glows bright blue, while malachite is green.

Baker looked closely at the mud found on the car. She also studied mud collected from the tire tracks. Baker learned something unusual about the soil at both places. It contained grains of two rare copper minerals called azurite and malachite.

Solving the Case

Baker learned an old copper mine was just upstream from the boat landing. She tested the soil at the mine. It also contained azurite and malachite. The minerals washed into the river, which carried them downstream.

Baker then tested dirt samples from other boat landings farther downstream. She found no azurite or malachite. The crime scene was the only landing with that combination of minerals. Baker's findings showed that the suspect's car must have been at the scene. He was found guilty and sentenced to prison.

Mud on the suspect's car matched the soil at the crime scene.

CHAPTER 2

Learn about:

- What makes up soil
- Collecting samples
- Comparing samples

Clues from the Earth

About 50,000 kinds of soils are found in the United States. Soil is more than just minerals, sand, and clay. It can include bits of leaves, fossils, plant stems, and pollen. Materials like paint flakes, concrete, and pieces of glass or brick are also found in soil.

Soil can link suspects to crime scenes in several ways. A killer who buries a body will disturb the soil with the shovel. As the killer digs, dirt can stick on his or her shoes or clothes. The tires and underside of the killer's car also pick up dirt.

◄ A shallow grave disturbs the soil.

Pieces of the Puzzle

CSIs collect dirt from the crime scene. They also take samples from nearby areas. Soil types can change within just a few feet.

Later, police may search a suspect's vehicle or home. They put large clumps of dirt in jars. They use tape to collect bits of dirt from clothing or furniture. When all the evidence is collected, police send it to a lab. That's where forensic geologists begin their work.

Jars and plastic bags hold soil
samples from crime scenes.

CHAPTER 3

Learn about:

- Locations and labels
- Looking for a match
- X-rays and microscopes

Science and Soil

Forensic geologists are most often asked to answer one question about a soil sample—whether it could have come from the crime scene. If it could, that is strong evidence against the suspect. If it could not, the suspect may be cleared.

Knowing where a sample came from is important. Geologists' findings wouldn't be legal to use in court without it. Every sample has a label showing the exact place where the soil was collected. Photos of the crime scene also help pinpoint the sample's location.

◀ Soil samples must be handled carefully.

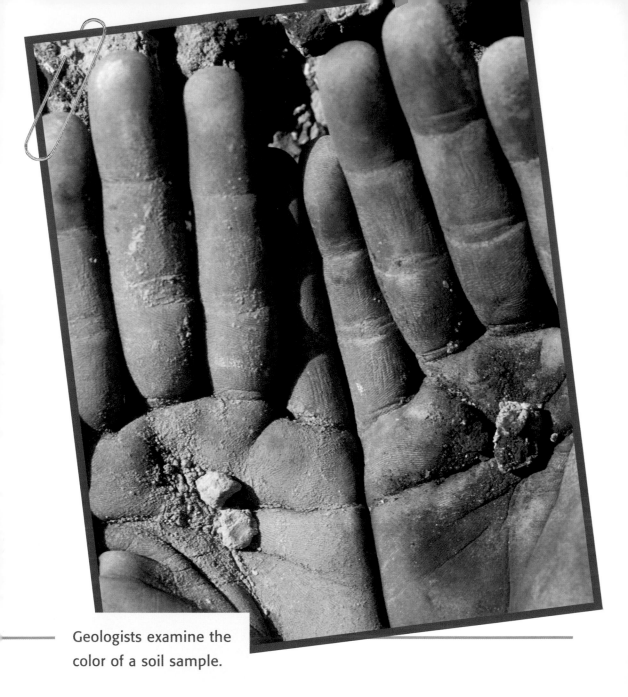

Geologists examine the color of a soil sample.

In the lab, geologists first look at soil color. If samples are not the same color, they might not come from the same area.

Next, geologists look at the soil's texture. If one sample is sandy and the other is claylike, there is no match. But even samples that seem similar might not be. Geologists need to look even deeper.

Layers of soil can have different colors and textures.

Tools of the Trade

Geologists examine samples that look alike under a microscope. They look for different kinds of rock and mineral particles. They compare the size of the particles. Some dirt contains glass pieces. Geologists use an instrument that measures the glass' features. These features can include the kind of glass, how fast light moves through the glass, and how dense the glass is.

Sometimes geologists take x-rays of a sample. The pattern x-rays make as they pass through a mineral can show what the mineral is. For example, both diamonds and graphite are made of carbon. Someone who looked only at the chemical makeup of the minerals might think they were the same. But the x-ray patterns would be very different.

Even when samples are similar, the geologist may say only that it is possible they came from the same place. Geologists can only be completely sure when both the crime scene soil and the sample share a unique feature. Still, forensic geologists have had amazing success helping police catch criminals.

◀ Geologists use microscopes
to compare samples.

CHAPTER 4

Learn about:

- A Mafia murder
- Nabbing a kidnapper
- Future of forensic geology

Closing the Case

A case from the early 1990s shows how soil evidence helps catch criminals. Five bodies were found in shallow graves on Staten Island, New York. The killings were connected to the Bonanno organized crime family.

Police arrested several members of the Bonanno family. They found a shovel with dirt on it at the home of one suspect. Police took soil samples from the gravesites. They took other samples near the gravesites. They drew maps showing the location of each sample.

An FBI forensic geologist tested all the samples. The dirt on the shovel closely matched the dirt from one gravesite. But the geologist knew that the suspect would probably say the dirt was from his garden. Next, the geologist took a sample from the garden. The garden dirt didn't match the dirt on the shovel. The evidence helped send two of the killers to prison.

◀ Joseph Bonanno led the Bonanno crime family.

Adolph Coors III was an owner of the Coors Brewing Company.

Coors Kidnapping

The information that geologists can uncover from clues in soil can be amazing. In 1960, business owner Adolph Coors III was kidnapped from his ranch near Morrison, Colorado.

Seven months later, hunters found Coors' body near Denver. Police suspected Joseph Corbett, who had been seen driving a yellow car near the Coors ranch. An alert FBI agent found the car burned at a dump in Atlantic City, New Jersey. It was more than 1,000 miles (1,600 kilometers) away from Colorado.

The Killer Carried a Hanky

Forensic geology helped solve a crime in Germany in 1904. A woman named Eva Disch was murdered. Police found a dirty handkerchief at the murder scene. The handkerchief contained bits of coal and a mineral called hornblende. It also held traces of chewing tobacco.

Police soon zeroed in on a suspect. He used chewing tobacco and had two jobs. One was at a place where coal was burned. The other was at a hornblende quarry. The suspect also had two layers of dirt on his pants. One layer matched the dirt at the crime scene. The other matched the dirt near Disch's house. When police told him of all the evidence, the suspect confessed.

The fire had destroyed any evidence inside the car, but there was still dirt under the fenders. Forensic geologists found the dirt was in four layers. The top layer matched the soil around the New Jersey dump. The next three layers came from the Rocky Mountains. One layer matched the mountains where Coors' body was found. Another matched the soil at the Coors ranch.

It was almost as if a record of Corbett's every move had been written on the underside of his car. The findings helped send Corbett to prison.

◀ Police arrested Corbett in November 1960.

Real and fake diamonds
can look very much alike.

Finding a Fake

Forensic geologists also work on forgery cases.
Some involve the sale of fake gems or copied
paintings. Geologists use fiber-optic lighting
and stereo binocular microscopes to study gems.

These tools show features in the gems that can't be seen with the naked eye.

Some artists are very skilled at making copies of famous paintings. But forensic geologists use microscopes and x-rays to study the paint. The paint sometimes contains materials made after the artwork was supposed to have been painted. That means the painting is a fake.

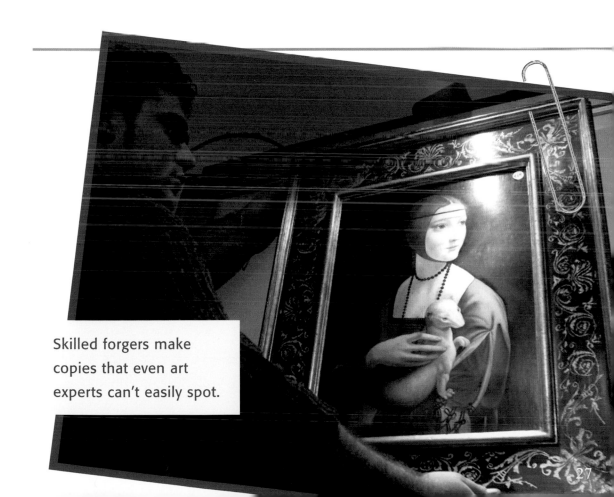

Skilled forgers make copies that even art experts can't easily spot.

A Box Full of Rocks

Geologists also work on theft cases. For example, a person orders diamonds or gold on the Internet. The package is sent through the mail or a delivery service. When the package arrives, it contains rocks instead. Where did the switch take place? A geologist could pinpoint the place along the delivery route where the rocks are found. The police can then search that area for the thief.

People are learning that geology can be a powerful tool for solving crimes. Geologists are now using improved x-ray instruments and scanning electron microscopes. These microscopes show differences between two particles in the same sample. With the new technology, forensic geologists will help police bring even more criminals to justice.

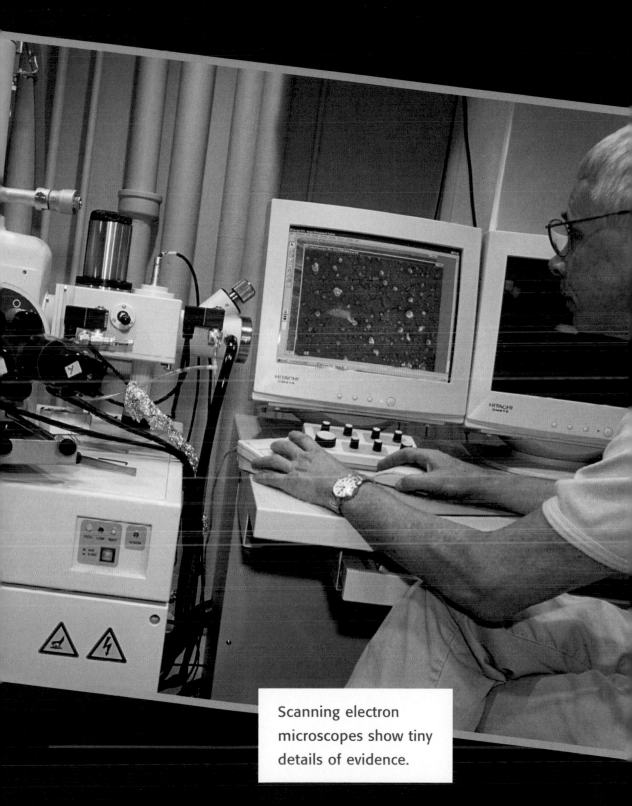

Scanning electron microscopes show tiny details of evidence.

Glossary

azurite (AAH-zyoo-rite)—a bright blue mineral that contains copper

element (EL-uh-muhnt)—a basic substance in chemistry that cannot be split into simpler substances

fiber optics (FYE-buhr OP-tiks)—thin pieces of glass or plastic that give off light

forgery (FORJ-ree)—the crime of making illegal copies of paintings, money, or other valuable objects

malachite (MAH-luh-kite)—a green mineral that contains copper; malachite is often used in jewelry.

mineral (MIN-ur-uhl)—a substance found in nature that is not made by a plant or animal

particle (PAR-tuh-kuhl)—a tiny piece of something

quarry (KWOR-ee)—a place where stone or other minerals are dug from the ground

Read More

Inserra, Rose. *Forensic Scientists*. Scientists at Work. North Mankato, Minn.: Smart Apple Media, 2004.

Pentland, Peter, and Pennie Stoyles. *Forensic Science*. Science and Scientists. Philadelphia: Chelsea House, 2003.

Rollins, Barbara B., and Michael Dahl. *Cause of Death*. Forensic Crime Solvers. Mankato, Minn.: Capstone Press, 2004.

Yount, Lisa. *Forensic Science: From Fibers to Fingerprints*. Milestones in Discovery and Invention. New York: Facts on File, 2007.

Internet Sites

FactHound offers a safe, fun way to find Internet sites related to this book. All of the sites on FactHound have been researched by our staff.

Here's how:

1. Visit *www.facthound.com*

2. Choose your grade level.

3. Type in this book ID **0736867872** for age-appropriate sites. You may also browse subjects by clicking on letters, or by clicking on pictures and words.

4. Click on the **Fetch It** button.

FactHound will fetch the best sites for you!

Index

cases
   Bonanno murders, 21
   Coors kidnapping, 22–23, 25
   Disch murder, 23
crime scene investigators (CSIs), 5,
      6, 7, 12
crime scenes, 5, 6, 9, 11, 12, 13, 15,
      19, 23

equipment
   fiber-optic lighting, 26
   scanning electron microscopes,
      28, 29
   stereo binocular microscopes,
      26–27
   x-rays, 19, 27, 28

forgery, 26–27
fossils, 11

labs, 12, 16

medical examiners (MEs), 5
minerals, 8–9, 11, 19, 23

photos, 6, 15

rocks, 7, 19, 28

soil
   collection, 6, 7, 8, 12, 15, 21
   colors, 16, 17
   textures, 17
   types, 11, 12
suspects, 6, 7, 9, 11, 12, 15, 21, 23

tire tracks, 5, 6, 8